MW00879493

PEDRO THE UGLIEST DOG IN THE WORLD

PAPA G

Copyright © 2011 by Papa G
Copyright © 2011 by BOOXTA
www.booxta.com
All rights reserved. No part of this book may be
reproduced or transmitted in any form or by any
electronic or mechanical means, including
photocopying, recording or by any information and
retrieval system, without the written permission of
the publisher and author, except where permitted by
law.
This novel is a work of fiction. Names,
characters, places and incidents are the product of
the author's imagination, or are used fictitiously.
Any resemblance to actual events, locales or persons,
living or dead, is purely coincidental.

ISBN: 978-1466449107

All rights reserved

This book is for Alexander, Gabrielle, Romana and Simba

Chapter 1—Hard knock Life

Pedro the ugliest dog in the world was ugly and when I say ugly, I don't mean just plain old dog ugly, I mean hideously and unfortunately ugly. He had two bug eyes—one big, one small. He had jutting teeth and wonky ears. He had a tongue that was precisely two inches too big for his mouth and apart from one tuft of spiky silver fur on top of his head he was completely bald. But if there is one thing a puppy can always count on—no matter how ugly he is—and that is the love of a mother, and Pedro's mother, a wise old goat hound by the name of Carmelita, loved Pedro with all her heart for the brave little soul he was.

"Why do I look so different from my brothers?" Pedro asked his mother one day.

"Because you are special." His mother gave him a reassuring lick.

"Special? Special how?" Pedro wanted to know.

"You are brave and strong, one day soon people will come and take you to join their pack and you will protect them with your life as this is a dogs duty, they will not care what you look like and they will love you for who you are."

"Who am I?" Pedro asked.

"You are the bravest little dog in the whole

of Mexico."

"Sweet!" Pedro shouted and wagging his little hairless tail went back to playing with his brothers.

Pedro enjoyed this time with his mother, and he enjoyed playing rough and tumble with his brothers. He even enjoyed the company of Señor Fuentes their owner.

Señor Fuentes was a kindly old man who walked with a limp. Carmelita had told her boys that Señor Fuentes was once a famous matador who got injured by a bull and had lost all his money chasing ladies. Señor Fuentes loved Carmelita dearly, and although he was very poor, he always made sure that she had enough to eat, so she in turn had enough milk for her puppies.

All too soon Señor Fuentes erected a wooden sign outside his little one room house. "Puppies for sale—twenty pesos," it said in bright red painted letters.

Pedro and his brothers were excited. "I wonder what kind of pack will choose me," they asked each other.

"Mine will be rich with a big house," said one.

"Mine will be pirates and we will sail the seven seas," said another.

"My pack will love me, and I will guard them with my life," Pedro said.

Pedro ran to his mother. "I will miss you, Mamma, when my pack comes to get me."

"I will miss you too, but this is the way of this world, and you will always be in my heart, my brave little puppy."

"And you will always be in mine," Later that day families came to look at the puppies. Children joyfully pointed out which puppy they would like to take home, and their parents paid Señor Fuentes twenty pesos. But none of the children pointed out Pedro. Some children laughed when they saw him and said things like, "That is one ugly dog," or "Ha-ha, look at his wonky ears." Other children cried, and one little girl was so scared she ran out of the house screaming.

One by one Pedro's brothers were taken, until by the end of that first day only Pedro remained.

"Why did no one take me, Mamma?" Pedro asked, his bottom lip trembling, tears forming in his little bug eyes.

Carmelita pushed Pedro's chin up and looked him in the eye. "Don't cry, Pedro; never cry, not because of the things people say. They are just words. They cannot hurt you. You are the bravest dog in the whole of Mexico, and the bravest dog in Mexico does not cry. Tomorrow is another day, and soon your pack will come for you."

But tomorrow came and went and so did the day after that, and no one took Pedro. Señor Fuentes changed his sign to fifteen pesos, then to ten pesos, then to five. Days turned into weeks, but no one came for Pedro. Señor Fuentes gave up trying to sell Pedro and changed his sign to read, "Free Puppy." People came again, but they did not want such a strange looking dog. They just laughed or cried or said mean things, but

Pedro did not cry, not once. He was the bravest dog in Mexico, and the bravest dog in Mexico did not cry.

More weeks went by. Eventually the sign fell down, and people stopped coming altogether. Pedro began to get worried.

"What are we going to do, Mamma? Señor Fuentes cannot afford to feed us both, and no one wants to take me."

Carmelita's shoulders sank but she managed to give Pedro a smile.

"Don't worry, Son, we can share my food. There will be enough, I'm sure."

Pedro felt a little better, and even though no one had chosen him, at least he would get to stay with his mamma.

Months went by, and even though there was not much food, Pedro got bigger and stronger and perhaps a little stranger looking. He was happy and did what he could around the house, which was mainly being a guard dog and barking at passers-by, Pedro was brave and loyal, and he would make sure his mother and Señor Fuentes were safe.

One day his mother called him.

"Pedro, my son, I am with puppies again. They will soon be born, and you will have more brothers and sisters."

"But we won't have enough food," Pedro said looking worried. "You will need extra food to grow them, and after they are born, you will need extra food to give them their milk."

His mother was tired, she pulled him close. "Don't worry; I am sure Señor Fuentes will provide somehow."

The next day Señor Fuentes came in and knelt beside Pedro's mother, giving her a pat. "Good news, old girl," he said, "I have found a nice family to take Pedro. I am going to borrow the neighbor's car and take him there this afternoon."

Carmelita was overjoyed and felt better than she had in weeks. "Pedro, Pedro, come quick; I have wonderful news."

Pedro came running in from the back yard. "What is it, Mamma?"

"Señor Fuentes has found you a pack at last; he is going to take you to them this very afternoon."

Pedro was so happy he could have cried, but he did not. "Oh Mamma, everything is going to be okay. You will have enough food for your puppies, and I will finally get what every dog wants— –a pack of his own."

"You will have a wonderful life my son. Remember to always be loyal and brave, and your pack will see you for who you really are— the real you inside, the bravest dog there ever was."

"Thank you, Mamma, I will."

It was not long before Señor Fuentes returned and put a leash on Pedro. He allowed Pedro one last good-bye to his mother.

"You will always be with me in my heart, Mamma," he said.

"And you in mine, Pedro. Remember always be brave and protect your pack with your life."

"I will Mamma, I promise." And with that, Señor Fuentes took Pedro, put him in the back of his neighbor's pickup, and drove off.

Oh, what a day this was for Pedro, getting his first ride in a car and finally getting to meet his pack. He was so happy. He stuck his head out of the side of the pickup and let his tongue flap around in the wind, spit flying everywhere. As Señor Fuentes drove out of town and turned towards the desert, Pedro was the happiest he had ever been.

After a couple of hours of driving down desert tracks, Señor Fuentes pulled the truck to a stop and got out. He untied Pedro. Pedro jumped down, his tail wagging; he couldn't wait to meet his pack. He wanted to leap about and bark, but instead he sat down and looked up at Señor Fuentes just like his mother had taught him. Señor Fuentes bent down and took Pedro's leash off. Pedro looked around. There was no house nearby, only desert, sand, and rocks as far as the eye could see. Confused, Pedro looked back at his master, but Señor Fuentes would not look at Pedro. Instead, he looked down at his shoes in shame and whispered, "*Lo siento*. Pedro." Pedro watched in shock as Señor Fuentes turned back towards the pickup. His master hesitated only a moment before he got in and drove off.

As Pedro watched the car disappear into the distance, he did not cry. It was hard, but he did not cry.

Chapter 2—The Desert

The desert was a strange place—nothing but sand and rocks—but it was also quiet and peaceful, a good place to think. And Pedro thought a lot that night. He thought about what Señor Fuentes had done to him, but he was not angry—at least now his mother would have enough food. But most of all he thought about what he should do. He needed to get out of the desert and quick. He decided that it was no good feeling sorry for himself. He was no longer a puppy. It was time to grow up and start standing up for himself. If his pack would not come to him, then he would just have to find them. After deciding what needed to be done, Pedro eventually curled up next to a rock and fell asleep just before sunrise.

"Hey, look, I found some road kill."

Pedro woke at the strange voice. A vicious looking brown wolf with a nasty scar where his nose should be, stood over him. Pedro jumped up pushing the wolf back.

Two other wolves sauntered over, one tall and skinny, the other short and fat "What you found, boss?"

"I found some road kill, but it's moving."

"Who are you calling road kill?" Pedro growled.

"You, you cockeyed spaniel! You look like you've been run over twice."

"Look who's talking. What happened to your snot nozzle? No nose." Pedro was outnumbered, but he wasn't going to go down without a fight.

No-Nose snarled, showing sharp teeth and black gums. "Oh, you are dead. We are going to rip you apart and leave your bones for the buzzards. Get him."

Pedro crouched low ready to pounce at whoever came at him first. "'You're the ones that will be torn apart."

The wolves hesitated and looked at each other. Like all bullies they were cowards. Pedro saw his chance to attack and was about to pounce, when a voice stopped him in his tracks.

"Hey, back off, chicken-lickers. Pick on someone your own size."

The wolves looked round in surprise, but could not see anyone.

"Who said that?" demanded No-Nose.

"Hey, down here, and I said back off."

Pedro didn't move, nor did he take his eyes off No-Nose.

The tall skinny wolf put his nose down to the sand to get a closer look, then jumped back as if something had bitten him. "It's a flea!" he screeched. If there is one thing furry animals don't like, it's fleas, and this was a big one.

"Get out of our way, flea," No-Nose growled. "Me and the boys are hungry, and one little flea aint gonna stop us from eatin this here dog."

"Yeah?" said the flea as he jumped up on the rock next to Pedro. "Well, I ain't no ordinary flea. I'm a Mexican jumping flea, heavy with eggs. If you or these other two fart wranglers take one more step towards this guy, me and my babies are going to bring some *pain* down on your furry behinds and when my babies come, they come with the hunger!"

The wolves looked at each other. The last thing they wanted was a flea infestation. They weren't that hungry. No-Nose backed away, his companions following. "We will get you, road kill; you see if we don't. You won't last two days in the desert, and when you start to weaken, that's when we will come for you."

"Whatever losers!" shouted the flea.

Pedro relaxed a little, but kept his eye on the departing wolves. "Thanks, but I can take care of myself," he said.

"Is that right?" said the flea. "Who is this dog that can take on three wolves on his own? You are either very brave or very dumb my friend."

"I am Pedro, and I am the bravest dog in the whole of Mexico."

"It is a pleasure to meet you Pedro- the bravest dog in the whole of Mexico. My Name is Dave."

"It is nice to meet you Dave"

"Pedro tell me, how exactly did you become the bravest dog in Mexico?"

Pedro gave this some thought. "I don't know, but I am. My mother told me so."

"Well, good for your mother, but those wolves were right about one thing—you will not survive alone in the desert."

"I will find a way."

"Sure you will. So, how did the bravest dog in Mexico end up in the middle of the desert anyhow?"

"I was dumped here by my master. I don't really want to talk about it."

Now that the wolves were out of sight, Pedro turned to where the flea was standing in order to get a closer look. The flea, although big for a flea, was still very small. He had two big black eyes, a jutting jaw with two large fangs and powerful looking legs. On his head he wore a sombrero, and slung over his back was a tiny guitar.

"Dumped hey? That sucks." Dave said.

"So what is a Mexican jumping flea doing in the middle of the desert?" Pedro asked.

"Oh, I was hitching a ride on a goat, but he didn't make it." A look of guilt flashed across Dave's face." We were on our way to Santa Maria"

"Santa Maria?"

"Yes, Santa Maria, it is a town where all animals are welcome, and they live in harmony, free of people. I was showing the goat how to get there, but ... Hey look Pedro, we could help each other out here. I need a ride, and you need to get out of the desert. I know this place like the back of my hand. If you let me stay in that fur on top of your head, I would be happy to show you the way to Santa Maria."

Pedro looked suspiciously at the flea. He did need some help, but he was unsure. "I don't know," he said. "What about your eggs?"

Dave laughed. "I haven't got any eggs. I'm a man-flea. Carrying eggs is woman's work. I just said that to scare off those mangy wolves."

Pedro laughed. He had never had a friend before, but he thought that maybe this flea could be a friend; he was quite brave after all. And how bad could having fleas be? Besides maybe he would find his pack in Santa Maria.

"Okay, it's a deal," Pedro said tilting his head so Dave could jump on. Dave didn't need asking twice. He jumped straight into Pedro's patch of spiky silver hair and started making himself at home.

"Hey, it's nice in here; smells good, too," he shouted.

"Good," said Pedro. "Now which way?"

"Erm ... just keep walking straight until I say."

"Right you are," said Pedro, setting off.

A moment later he felt a sharp pain on top of his head. "Yeeouch!" he cried. "Hey, what are you doing in there?"

"Don't worry about that, just keep walking," came a muffled reply.

Pedro wondered if having fleas was such a good idea after all.

Chapter 3—Desperate
Three days later

"We should have been there by now." Pedro was crawling through the sand, the unrelenting sun beating down on him. He hadn't had a drink in three days; he was half dead, and things were desperate. "I'm not going to make it."

"Well, if you had gone straight ahead like I said, we would be in Santa Maria by now," Dave said from his furry home.

"What? I *have* been walking straight for three days!" Pedro fell flat on his face exhausted. "You don't know where we are going, do you?" he croaked. "This is what happened to that goat you were on, wasn't it? Now I am going to die as well, and you will just sit here, waiting for the next sucker to come along and give you a lift."

"How dare you? I know this desert like the back of my hand, and I am sure we are nearly there. Besides you have got plenty to drink all around you."

Pedro looked up. "Where?"

"The cactus ... they are full of water."

Pedro was gobsmacked; he couldn't believe he was nearly dead, and Dave hadn't said a thing before.

"But ... but why didn't you tell me before?"

"Well, I was kind of hoping we would find something better—an oasis or something, you know with fresh water, maybe some fruit, and oh yeah, lady fleas or even better ticks"

Pedro was too exhausted to argue; instead he used the last of his strength to drag himself to the nearest cactus.

"Now carefully use those wonky teeth of yours to pierce some holes," Dave instructed.

Pedro bit down on the firm green flesh, and a clear liquid ran out. Pedro lapped at the cactus juice, unconcerned for the prickles.

"Oh, that's good," Pedro said, and then bit some more holes.

"Hey, save some for me," Dave said as he left his hairy lair for the first time in three days and crawled to the end of Pedro's nose.

"I love this stuff, it makes my head go funny,"

"Funny? Funny how?"

"This is the El Loco cactus. It sends you crazy."

Crazy sounded better than dead to Pedro, so he kept drinking.

Chapter 4—Night Giraffes

Pedro lay on his back with his legs in the air. "Hahahahahahahah, hooooooohoooooohooooooh, hehehheheehehehehehehhe, ohhhh, Dave man, you are the best flea a dog ever had, I love you."

Dave and Pedro had been laughing non-stop for three hours. The cactus juice had indeed sent them crazy, and as they gazed at the night sky, the stars twirled and spun, like fireworks on Independence Day.

"I love you too, Pedro," Dave had been on many animals in his life, but he had never really been friends with any of them. They considered him an annoyance, and he thought of them as little more than a convenience. But there was something he liked about this funny looking dog.

"You can live on my head forever," Pedro said

"Thanks, I intend to." Then their laughter continued as they watched the display they thought the sky was putting on for them.

Another hour passed.

"Hahahahahahahah, hooooooohoooooohooooooh, hehehheheehehehehehehhe,   ohhhh....   I'm hungry," Pedro said still staring at the stars with big bug eyes.

"Yeah, me too."

"No, I'm really hungry. I could eat a horse. Let's go hunting; there must be something to eat round here somewhere," Pedro said.

"Sure there is. Did I ever tell you I am an expert animal tracker?"

"No, that is so cool." Pedro got unsteadily to his feet.

Dave peered out from the fur on Pedro's head. "Well, of course I am; I'm a flea. Now shhhhhhhh, we don't want to scare any unsuspecting beasts that may be nearby. We need to find a trail or something."

After half an hour or so of stumbling around and giggling in the dark, Pedro put his nose to the ground and started sniffing. "Hey, look at this Dave. What is it?"

Dave scrambled to the front of his hairy hideaway to take a look. "Aha! It's a poo," he said, then took a sharp intake of breath. "Not just any ordinary poo either. That's a giraffe poo!"

"Get out of here, you nut case. There's no giraffes in the desert," Pedro said, not believing one word of it.

"Maybe not, but that is definitely a giraffe poo."

"How can you tell?" Pedro asked, giving it another sniff and screwing up his nose.

"Well, it's flat for one thing."

"Right …" Pedro said looking confused.

"And it's round for another."

"That don't mean a thing," Pedro said

"No? Really? Well, when I was a small child, the old women of the village would gather to sing the giraffe poo song." Then Dave got out his guitar and began singing loudly.

Because a giraffe is extremely tall,
It's a very long way for a poo to fall.
Instead of being nice and round
And piled neatly upon the ground,
A giraffe poo is completely flat
And lands on the ground with a mighty splat.

Dave finished his song with an impressive guitar solo, then he and Pedro howled with laughter

Another hour went by.

"Hahahahah, hoooooooo ... Okay, let's get that giraffe," Pedro said with tears running down his cheeks.

Pedro and Dave stumbled after the trail of poo, giggling and shushing each other, and eventually coming to a rusty old fence. Pedro crouched down. "Look, there it is," he whispered, wide eyed, pointing to a large four-legged animal grazing on the other side.

"Yeah man, I told you. Now go and eat it, but be quiet," Dave whispered back, trying to stifle his giggles.

Pedro climbed over the rusty fence and started sneaking through the dry grass, keeping low, moving slowly towards the unsuspecting creature. When he got within striking distance, Pedro pounced, digging his sharp wonky teeth hard into the creature's rear.

"Yeeeoowww," a shaggy goat cried out in shock, turning round to see a hideous looking animal with big black eyes hanging off his behind. "What the fluff ... what do you think you're doing?" the goat screamed at Pedro.

"Oh sorry, I thought you were a giraffe," Pedro slurred through his mouthful of furry goat butt.

"Help ... Help ... Help me! I'm being eaten ... alive!" the terrified goat screeched, running around, bucking his legs in an attempt to shake Pedro off. Pedro hung onto the goat's butt like a demented pit-bull. Dave was screaming, "Let go man, it's a goat."

From the dark an angry voice shouted, "Hey!"

Pedro looked up just in time to see a large rock just before it smacked him in the face.

Chapter 5—Bonita

Pedro woke with a pounding headache. He was lying on a clean bed of straw in a small white room. The bright morning sun was coming through an open window. Sitting by the door was the most beautiful Chihuahua Pedro had ever seen, with beautiful big brown eyes, shiny brown fur, and a perfect wet nose.

"Are you an angel?" he asked quietly.

The Chihuahua looked up surprised "N…n…n…no," she stammered. "My name is Bonita."

"What a beautiful name," Pedro said. He began to rise, rubbing a paw over his throbbing head. "It is a pleasure to meet you. My name is Pedro."

Bonita got to her feet "Papá ... Papá come quickly. El Chupacabra is awake," she shouted.

"El Chupawhatnow?" Pedro said, confused.

The Chihuahua came closer and pointed a paw at Pedro. "Papá and Señor Hables caught you last night trying to eat our goat."

"Oh, that," Pedro said a little embarrassed. "I can explain that. I drank some loco cactus that made my head go weird, and I thought it was a giraffe."

"I heard you were crazy. Papá ... Papá," Bonita called again.

"I'm not crazy. Dave will tell you. It was the cactus."

"Dave!" He shouted, but Dave was busy snoring.

"Who is this Dave? There is no one else here. You are crazy," Bonita edged closer to the door.

Just then it burst open. Bonita's Papá came barging in "Get back, foul beast," the older Chihuahua growled.

Pedro backed away. "What's going on?"

"What's going on? I will tell you what is going on El Chupacabra. I caught you in the act of sucking my goat."

"I already explained that," Pedro interrupted, but the Chihuahua bared his teeth and continued shouting.

"I am the Mayor of Santa Maria, and I have only spared you as this is our way. We live in peace and respect one another here. How dare you come here and suck our goats."

Pedro lowered his head "I am very sorry, I didn't mean to cause any trouble. Please let me make it up to you somehow."

The mayor paused and gave it some thought. "Our town could possibly use the help of El Chupacabra. If you agree to help us. We may give you a second chance. But if not, I will have you locked away for good!"

With that he pushed Bonita out of the room, locking the door behind them.

"And they think I'm crazy. Dave, wake up!" he yelled.

"Hey, don't shout. My head is killing me," Dave answered in a groggy voice.

"We're in trouble. We are being held prisoner by a mad mayor and his crazy but beautiful daughter." Pedro went over to the window to find an escape route. The window, looking out over a town square, was high up— too high to climb out.

Pedro looked out over Santa Maria, the entire town was made out of giant cactuses with windows and doors cut into them. Milling about were all kinds of animals, going about their daily business—owls, porcupines, tortoises and armadillos.

"Wow" Pedro said wide eyed.

"Yeah, it's pretty cool, hey?" Dave said, getting ready for breakfast.

"Ouch..." Pedro scratched his head. "Look, they keep calling me El Chupacabra. What does that mean?"

Dave jumped at the name. "EL Chupacabra!" he shouted. "Aye, aye, yay, this is not good."

"Why? What is it?" Pedro asked.

Dave started to explain. "El Chupacabra is a hideously ugly blood-sucking monster that eats goats. El Chupacabra means *goat sucker*!" Dave jumped down from Pedro's head onto the window sill. "In the village I lived in as a small child, El Chupacabra used to come at night to suck the goats and terrify everyone with his hideous ugliness. The old women of the village used to gather to sing about it." Dave cleared his throat. "Ahem." He got his guitar ready.

El Chupacabra is the fruit of the Devil.

He is completely, completely evil.
He'll steal your children and eat your cat,
But it is much, much worse than that.
He hides in dark places under your bed.
He'll suck your goats until they are dead
And then he'll ...

"Whoa, whoa," Pedro interrupted. "You mean to say that Bonita thinks I am some kind of monster?"

"Yes, a hideously ugly, goat-sucking monster."

Pedro put his head in his paws. He couldn't believe it, the first girl he had ever met thought he was a hideous monster.

"I need to tell Bonita the truth," Pedro said. "Her father said they needed help. I will help them in any way I can."

"What do think they want you to do?" Dave asked.

"I don't know," Pedro said scratching the side of his head and looked out over the town. "Look there, in the middle of the square, they are digging a well." Pedro pointed to a half-built well with a pile of dirt next to it. "That must be what he meant. Every town needs a well. I will show Bonita what a good digger I am, and then she will like me." Pedro carefully picked Dave up and put him back on his head, then lay back down and spent the morning thinking of Bonita and his pounding headache.

Chapter 6—Poor Nigel

Around midday Bonita came in carrying a small pale of water. Pedro stayed on his bed trying his best not to frighten her. "I am not a monster,"

Bonita placed the water on the floor next to the bed "Try telling that to Nigel,"

Pedro was confused. "Nigel?"

"Our goat! Papá has been up half the night with him. Nigel just sits there rocking backwards and forwards saying, "El Chupacabra" over and over again. He hasn't blinked in eight hours, not once."

"I am really sorry about that," Pedro said, ashamed. "I wasn't going suck his blood or anything. Let me make it up to you. Let me help your town, and you will see that I am not the monster you think I am."

"You will help us?" Bonita said, surprised.

"Yes, I have made a fool of myself, and this is the least I can do."

Bonita began to cry. "Thank you, oh, thank you, that means so much to me. I must tell Papá. He will be very, very happy. He will tell the townsfolk, and they will be very, very happy, too." Bonita licked Pedro on the cheek and ran out of the room.

Pedro was stunned.

"Wow! What a weirdo." Dave said. "By the time you dig that well, she will want to get married or something."

Pedro just sat there with a silly look on his face and his tongue hanging out.

Chapter 7—The Town Meeting

Word got around that the mayor had caught El Chupacabra, and everyone gathered for the town meeting. The crowd chatted excitedly under the balcony of the mayor's cactus house. "I hear he is so ugly, if you look at him, you will turn to stone," said an aardvark.

"I heard that his eyes glow red in the dark and that he is completely insane," said a squirrel in reply.

"I heard he ate his own fluffing mother," a frightened looking owl said.

The mayor came out and called for quiet. "Yes, it is true I have captured El Chupacabra," The crowd gasped in horror. The mayor carried on "I have to report that El Chupacabra is ... well, not as bad or as crazy as you may have heard. In fact he seems rather nice."

The crowd started murmuring loudly, and the mayor called for quiet again. "I am pleased to say that El Chupacabra has agreed to help us"

The crowd couldn't believe it. They all started shouting questions at once, and the mayor called for calm once more. "I will bring El Chupacabra out to meet you all shortly, but first questions. One at a time though, please."

A large tortoise towards the back raised a front leg.

"Yes, Señor Tortoise," the mayor said.

"Will El Chupacabra steal my children?" he asked.

"No, no of course not" the mayor assured him.

"Will he eat my cat?" an aardvark shouted.

The mayor looked unsure and turned to where Pedro was waiting. "Will you be eating any cats?" he asked from the corner of his mouth.

"No!" an indignant Pedro said.

The mayor turned to the gathered town. "There will be no cat eating." A small ripple of applause broke out.

An owl put up his wing.

"One last question," the mayor said.

"Is it true that El Chupacabra sucks goats?"

The mayor looked down and slowly nodded his head. "Yes, yes, it is true," he said.

Pedro's cheeks burned in embarrassment.

"BUT," the mayor shouted above the chatter, "you will all be pleased to know that Nigel is feeling much better now, and the doctor is sure that he will be able to blink again soon. He is none the worse for the sucking that he got."

Then the mayor gestured to Pedro. "And here he is, the one, the only El Chu-pa-cabra! Who also likes to be known as Pedro."

Pedro stepped out onto the balcony.

"Wave to the crowd," an excited Dave whispered.

Pedro gave an uneasy wave and said, "I have come to help you." The crowd erupted, cheering and whooping with joy. Pedro kept waving.

Dave was jumping up and down on Pedro's head. "Haha," he shouted, "this town is nuts! They are crazy over this well."

"Wells are important," Pedro said, enjoying the attention.

The mayor called for silence again. "I declare today to be El Chupacabra Day, and tonight we will have a big fiesta with Pedro as the guest of honour." The crowd went doubly wild, and everyone, everyone was deliriously happy.

Chapter 8—The Fiesta

The dusty town square was decorated with strings of desert flowers and prickly pears. A long table carved from a dried cactus stood at the centre. Señor Hables a middle aged anteater was running around catching locusts with his long sticky tongue, before skewering them onto sticks that he placed onto an open fire to cook. The whole town was there, and they greeted Pedro warmly, thanking him for helping them.

Dave had decided that with so many furry animals around he should keep quiet for the evening for fear of being swatted. Pedro was happy to make small talk with the townspeople, but was keeping an eye out for Bonita. He was determined to tell her about the mistaken identity and tomorrow he would start digging the well to show her what a good dog he really was.

When Bonita arrived, Pedro excused himself from the aardvark that he had been chatting with and went straight over to her. "You look fantastic,"

"Why thank you, Pedro," Bonita said, fluttering her eye lashes.

The mayor climbed onto the table to get everyone's attention. "Animals and avians, if you would kindly take your places Señor Hables tells me the food is almost ready."

Pedro took his place as guest of honor between the mayor and Bonita. "Pedro, let me get you a drink," the mayor said, pushing over a bowl of water. "It has been a long time since our town has had something to celebrate. After dinner we have music, Señor Squirrel is a wonderful singer, and there will be as many locusts as you can eat.

"Locusts?" Pedro said.

"Yes, Santa Maria is famous for its roasted locusts, it is our speciality. They are attracted to firelight so there is plenty to eat."

Pedro shuddered as the freshly roasted locusts arrived, then turned to Bonita. "Perhaps later you could show me around your wonderful town?"

Bonita smiled. "I would love to, Pedro,"

The mayor, Bonita, and Pedro happily chatted throughout the meal, and then listened to Señor Squirrel sing a wonderful rendition of *La Bamba*. When Señor Squirrel had finished, Pedro and Bonita stood and excused themselves.

"My father founded Santa Maria three years ago" Bonita said as they began their walk "My parents and I were abandoned in the Desert by our masters. My mother was unwell and didn't make it...the sun was too much for her and we couldn't find water."

"I am sorry" Pedro said.

Bonita took a deep breath and continued "Señor Hables found us soon after we had buried her, we were near death ourselves. He brought us here for was food and water. When Papá saw the giant cactus, he decided there and then to make it not only our home, but a haven for all animals, lost, abandoned or just wanting a better way of life, he named it Santa Maria after my mother.

"Your father is a great dog"

Pedro stopped Bonita and looked her in the eyes; he needed to tell her the truth. "Bonita I need to..." Just then a bell started ringing, someone screamed, and a squirrel started shouting, "*Banditos*, banditos, the banditos are coming."

Pedro looked around "Quick, hide. The banditos are coming." But through all the commotion Bonita had not heard. She gave him a quick lick. "You are so brave," she said.

"What?" Pedro yelled as everyone ran to hide.

"When you have taken care of the banditos, our town can get back to normal, and we will be happy again. Good luck, Pedro."

"Who are these banditos?" he demanded.

"They work for the Lizard King—Gary Gecko and his gang. They come once a week to take food and supplies. If they keep coming, we will not have enough once the locust season ends. But now you are here, we will be okay. They will be no match for El Chupacabra."

As the truth of the situation dawned on Pedro, he barely noticed Bonita running off. When he looked round, Pedro and Dave were alone.

"Hey, I think she really likes you," Dave said.

"Great, I find a girl who doesn't think I'm the ugliest dog in the world just before I die at the hands of a blood-thirsty gang of banditos."

"Don't worry about it. You are El Chupacabra," Dave said

"But I'm not," Pedro said staring toward the edge of town as the banditos came into sight.

"Yeah, but they don't know that, and you are the bravest dog in Mexico," Dave said moving towards Pedro's ear. "I have a plan."

Chapter 9—Banditos

There were ten lizards that rode into town that night, each one meaner looking than the next. Eight were riding on big black hairy tarantulas, with another two riding on a canvas covered wagon pulled by four massive rats. They rode hard, kicking up a mighty dust cloud, whooping and a hollering as they came. When they got to the town square, they pulled their tarantulas to a halt.

"What is that?" Gary Gecko shouted, seeing Pedro standing there bold as brass.

"Dunno, boss, but it sure is ugly," a lizard mounted on a particularly nasty looking spider replied.

"Hey, butt-face," Gecko called out, "you must be as dumb as you are ugly, standing in our way like that. Now git before we set our spiders on yer."

Pedro moved towards the lizard gang.

"Now remember what I said Pedro, act real crazy," Dave whispered as Pedro got closer.

"Phew! Man you are so ugly. You'd make an onion cry," Gecko said, and the lizard gang started laughing.

"Hey, you are so ugly, when you was born, the doctor slapped your mother," a thin lizard on the wagon shouted. The lizards laughed so much they almost fell off their spiders.

Pedro stood there and waited. When the laughter died down a little, he said, "Okay, who's first?"

Gary Gecko sneered. "First for what boy?"

"First to have their brains sucked by El Chupacabra!" Pedro said, then howled at the moon with a crazy look in his eye. "Hooooooooooooo-wooow-wooooo."

The lizards' eyes went wide in terror. "El ... El ... El Chupacabra?" Gary stammered, the color draining from his face. "We did not know it was you," he said, trying to smile.

"Really," Pedro said casually, walking up to Gecko's spider. He smacked it square in the face. The big spider hissed and jerked.

"Yes, really. I did not know it was you ... I am very sorry about that onion thing," Gecko said, worried about what El Chupacabra might do to him.

"And I am really sorry that I talked about your mother that way," the lizard on the wagon said, terrified that he was going to be first to get a brain sucking.

"Really," Pedro said jumping onto the wagon and biting down on the frightened lizard's tail, giving it a vicious shake. "Owowow! Please don't hurt me," the lizard pleaded.

Pedro jumped down and confronted Gecko again. 'So what should I do with you?" He said glaring at the shaking lizard with his crazy bug eyes.

"You could just let us go, and we can just forget about all this," He said hopefully.

"It was just a case of mistaken identity ... it won't happen again."

Pedro smacked the spider in the face again. This time the big spider reared up, and Gary Gecko struggled to control it.

"Hey, don't go too far," Dave whispered in Pedro's ear. "Just tell them to get out of town."

"Okay," Pedro snarled, "I will let you off this time, but if I ever see any of you streaks of snot again, I will suck every last one of you *dry*! Muahahahah. Now get outa town before I change my mind."

"Thank you, Señor El Chupacabra sir," the relieved lizard on the wagon said.

"You will not regret this," Gary Gecko said, not believing his luck, then they turned and left town even quicker than they arrived.

Pedro whooped with joy. His heart was pounding furiously. He couldn't believe he had pulled it off.

"Haha! You did it!" Dave shouted almost as relieved as Pedro.

Bonita came running to Pedro. "You are so brave," she said.

Behind her came the mayor and the rest of the town, cheering. They hoisted Pedro into the air and danced around the square singing "El Chupacabra, El Chupacabra, he is a hero."

"Yeah!" Pedro shouted above the cheering. "Being El Chupacabra *rocks*."

Chapter 10—The Lizard King

"What do you mean? El Chupa-fluffing-cabra! Where are my supplies?" the Lizard King shouted as Gary Gecko and his gang kneeled, shaking on the floor of their cave hideout. The large iguana got off his throne carved from the rock and walked around the smaller lizards cowering on the floor. The Lizard King was a frightening sight with only one eye and a long jagged scar running down his face.

"El Chupacabra! He is at the town, and he told us that if he ever sees us again, he will suck us all ... dry!" Gary Gecko explained.

The Lizard King pulled Gary Gecko to his feet. "Tell me, did this El Chupacabra have eyes that glowed like fire?"

"No," Gecko replied.

"*No*!" the Lizard King screamed. "And tell me, was he completely insane?"

"Well, he kept smacking my spider's face," the smaller lizard said.

"Hmm, that is kind of crazy," the Lizard King agreed. "But was he twice as big as you with claws like knives and teeth as long as your finger? Did he have two horns about his head and have a black forked tongue? Did he smell so bad you wanted to pull off your own noses? Did he shriek and scream until your ears popped? And did he in fact eat anyone's brains or suck their blood?"

"Err, no," Gecko replied.

"Then this is not El Chupacabra," the Lizard King said.

Just then No-Nose came running into the cave with fatty and skinny following close behind.

"And where have you fur brained twonks been hiding?" The Lizard King bellowed.

"Sorry master, we were out looking for food" No-Nose said bowing his head.

"So where is it then?"

"Well we thought we had found some road kill but it turned out to be this really ugly dog with fleas"

"An ugly dog you say" the Lizard King shook his head "I am surrounded by idiots...get back out there and don't come back empty handed again or I will make you monkey touchers regret it!"

The Lizard King turned back to Gary Gecko "El Chupacabra is in an insane asylum up north. We shall tell him about this pretender and bring him here to deal with him."

"But how do you know this?" Gecko asked.

"Because El Chupacabra, shall we say, is a friend of mine." The Lizard King stroked his long, jagged scar. "And it pays to know where your friends are"

"But how can we get him out if he is locked up in an insane asylum?" Gecko asked.

"Oh, he only stays there because he likes it."

"But will it be safe?" a thin lizard asked.

"Probably not," said the king smiling.

The Lizard King motioned to his men to get up. "Now go and bring me the real El Chupacabra."

Chapter 11—The Next Morning

The mayor came and woke Pedro up at eight the next morning. The celebrations had gone on late into the night, and much food and drink had been consumed with everyone toasting the hero of the hour. Pedro had spent most of his time trying to get to speak with Bonita, but it was hard when everyone wanted to shake his paw, thanking El Chupacabra for saving their town.

"Good morning, Pedro." The mayor pushed open the shutters, letting in the bright morning light.

"Good morning, mayor," Pedro said opening one eye.

"It is a beautiful day, and it is all thanks to you. You have run off the Lizard King's gang, and they will not be back while El Chupacabra is here. You will stay here as my guest for as long as you like. Come and take breakfast with me and Bonita out on the veranda, and we shall discuss your new job."

"New job?"

"Yes, the town got together early this morning and voted that you should be our new sheriff. You will accept, won't you, Pedro? It is a great honor."

Pedro sat up. "Err, of course," he said before he could think it through.

"Good," said the mayor. "Then it is settled. With El Chupacabra as our sheriff, no one will ever cause trouble in Santa Maria again."

Pedro let out a deep sigh as the mayor shut the door.

"Hoo-hoo-hoo," Dave said from the top of Pedro's head. "Man, you are getting yourself in deep here, Pedro."

"What? It was your idea to pretend to be El Chupacabra."

"Yeah, but only to the bandits. I never said to lie to the whole town and especially not to Bonita. ladies don't like to be lied to, Pedro."

"I suppose no one does. I will tell her the truth. She will understand . . . I hope,"

***

As Pedro arrived for breakfast, Bonita smiled and said, "Good morning, Sheriff. We have freshly roasted locusts, hot from the fire"

Pedro scanned the food spread out for them. "Mmm, locusts again! My favorite." He lied.

"Sit, Pedro, enjoy." The mayor took his place.

Pedro, Bonita, and the mayor laughed and joked about the night before as they ate, and Pedro blushed when they talked about how brave he was. All the while Pedro was trying to pick a good time to tell them the truth, but before he knew it, breakfast was over, and the mayor was excusing himself.

"I must get on. I have a lot to do," he said as he got up.

"Pedro, come with me. We have much to discuss about your duties as sheriff, and we need to get you your sheriff's hat and badge.

"Of course, mayor," Pedro said standing up.

Pedro turned to Bonita. "I have something I really need to tell you."

"You will have to tell me later. You shouldn't keep Papá waiting"

"Come. Pedro," the mayor shouted from the hallway.

"When can you meet me?" Pedro asked.

"How about Friday night, in the town square. There is music and plenty of locusts to eat. It can be our first date."

"Date!" Pedro said, his eyes going wide.

"Yes, you do want to date me, don't you, Sheriff Pedro?" Bonita smiled.

"Oh, yes please," Pedro spluttered.

Bonita giggled as she walked away.

Chapter 12—The Asylum

The large stone insane asylum stood at the edge of the desert. Animals that had caught mental were treated and sometimes locked away there. Gary Gecko had drawn the short straw. The other lizards waited anxiously outside while he walked down a dark staircase to the basement. It smelt damp, and screaming could be heard in the distance. A nurse—a middle aged owl—looked Gecko up and down

"Doctor Jose, you say the president himself has sent you to study him?"

"Yes, El Presidente wants to know just how crazy he is," Gecko lied.

"Oh, he's crazy alright, crazy insane," the owl said as they reached the basement. "We keep him in the last cell on the left." She gestured down a dimly lit hallway lined by a row of five cells. A thick white line was painted down the middle of the floor. "When you talk to him, always look him in the eye and do *not* cross the white line. Whatever he says or whatever he does, do *not* cross over the white line. He cannot reach you if you stay on the right side of the line."

Gecko hesitated. "Aren't you coming with me?" he asked.

"I might work in an asylum, Doctor, but I'm not crazy," the owl said. "If you want him, you're welcome to him, but you will have to go and get him. When you are done, just call and we will make the arrangements."

Gecko looked down the hallway and then back to the Owl.

"Go on then, Doctor. You won't be able to study him from here," the nurse said and walked away.

Gecko started down the hallway, keeping as far to the right as possible. All the cells were dark, and Gecko could not see beyond the thick metal bars. He was unsure if anyone was in them. From one cell he thought he heard giggling and from another maybe crying, but he could not be sure. As he reached the last cell, he hesitated. It smelled terrible. Gary Gecko was almost too scared to look. He inched a little closer.

"El … El … El Chupacabra?" he said, but no answer came. He got closer still, and there at the back of the dimly lit cell, two red, unblinking eyes glowed like hot coals. He could hear a deep rumbling growl.

"El Chupacabra?" Gecko repeated.

An ear piercing shriek came from the monster, and it threw itself at metal bars. Gecko jumped back as El Chupacabra reached through the bars snarling, growling, spit flying everywhere. Gary was terrified as he looked at the creature. It was hideous. It looked like a cross between a wolf and a pig, with a short powerful snout and teeth like a shark. Long, vicious claws reached and swiped at the terrified lizard.

"The Lizard King sent me," Gecko squealed, squeezing his eyes shut.

El Chupacabra pulled back and stood calm as if nothing had happened.

"The Lizard King you say. I knew him once; he had a delicious eye."

"He asks that you come to the desert," Gecko said.

"What for?" El Chupacabra asked suspiciously. "I like it here. It's quiet and dark. I can hear my voices nice and clear. Besides the food's not bad. Why should I leave all this to come to the desert? The desert makes me crazy. There are too many goats there."

Gecko looked down checking the white line. "In Santa Maria there is someone protecting them who claims he is El Chupacabra."

"*What*!" El Chupacabra screamed, going into a rage even worse than before. He started jumping up and down, his eyes glowing redder than ever. Gecko thought that steam may come out of ears.

"*Aaaarrrgghhhh! Mother fluffer I will rip him to pieces and eat his brains. There is only one El Chupacabra, and that is me....me, me, me!*"

Squishing himself as far to the right as possible, Gary Gecko looked on horrified as the creature bounced off walls, tearing every piece of furniture in his cell to tiny pieces. The small lizard had never seen anything like it before. Not even the Lizard King was anything near as scary as El Chupacabra. Suddenly the monster stopped screaming, his chest heaving.

"Tell the owl I'm leaving," he said.

Gecko, open mouthed, nodded and ran back to where the owl was waiting.

He panted trying to catch his breath. "We'll take him."

"Not a problem," the relieved owl said.

"I don't suppose you have a straight jacket, some soap, some rope, and maybe some big sticks?" Gecko asked.

Chapter 13—Tasty Eyes

"So we meet again." The Lizard King got up from his throne.

El Chupacabra was in a wheelchair, loops and loops of rope bound his body, legs, and arms, a wire muzzle covered his face. Still the Lizard King approached carefully.

"Release me!" El Chupacabra demanded. "I have come to deal with the one who pretends to be El Chupacabra. I will make him regret the day he was born."

"All in good time El Chupacabra."

The Lizard King looked over to the lizard gang. There were only four of them left, and they were covered in cuts and bruises.

"What happened?" he demanded.

Gary Gecko stepped forward. "We had some trouble. We lost some lizards along the way, and some goats were harmed." Gecko's bottom lip quivered a little. "It was awful," he murmured.

The Lizard King slapped him before he could cry. He turned back to El Chupacabra. "I see you still have a taste for goats."

"Goats and lizard eyes." El Chupacabra smiled.

"Enough!" the Lizard King shouted, rubbing his scar. "Get the spiders ready. Tonight we ride."

Chapter 14—The Hot Date

Pedro arrived in the town square shortly after nightfall. The square was busy, Señor Squirrel wandered around serenading couples that sat beside small fires that dotted the town square.

"So are you going to tell her?" Dave shouted down from the rim of Pedro's new sheriff hat.

"Yes," Pedro whispered from the corner of his mouth. "Now keep quiet."

Across the square Pedro spotted Bonita talking with Señor Hables. Feeling nervous, Pedro adjusted his sheriff badge as he watched her. He was uncertain how she would react when she found out he was just a dog, but he knew he had to tell her the truth. Bonita looked up, excused herself, and made her way over.

"Well, don't you look fine with your sheriff hat and badge," Bonita said. She leant over and gave Pedro a gentle lick on the cheek. "Come, let us sit" Bonita said smiling at how stunned Pedro looked.

Pedro shook his head, managing to compose himself. "Sure," he said, as they took a seat next to a vacant fire.

For a short while Pedro and Bonita were happy sitting together, chatting and roasting locusts. Pedro wanted the evening to go on forever, but he had to tell Bonita the truth.

"I have something I have to tell you,"

Bonita smiled, but she could see he was troubled. "What is it?"

Pedro stared into the flames "I am not sure how to say this."

"What?"

"I am not who you think I am," Pedro said at last.

Bonita looked relieved and let out a short laugh. "I know that."

"You do?" Pedro spluttered in surprise.

"Of course, everyone thinks El Chupacabra is evil and nasty, but I know that you are kind and brave."

Pedro's shoulders slumped. "That's not what I mean. I am not ..."

Just then a loud scream pierced the night air; Pedro looked up and could see the other animals staring in horror at something behind him.

He slowly looked around, and there stood the Lizard King with his gang.

Chapter 15—Know When to Fold Them

"So you are El Chupacabra?" The Lizard King sneered. "And I see they have made you sheriff. Why, that is priceless. Sheriff El Chupacabra."

Pedro stood frozen, not sure what to do. He was out numbered, and the Lizard King was a fearsome sight.

"You are going to have to bluff them again, Pedro," Dave whispered in his ear.

"Yeah, I know. I guess one last time won't hurt," Pedro replied.

Pedro pushed the brim of his hat up and looked the Lizard King square in the eye. "You and your slimy friends have until the count of three before I go all crazy on you and start sucking some lizards."

"Is that so, El Chupacabra?" The Lizard King laughed and clapped which kind of worried Dave.

"Erm, Pedro," Dave said.

"Shhhh, I'm busy," he replied. "*One!*" Pedro shouted across the square.

"Ooh, quick boys, let's get out of town before the monster of Mexico comes over here and starts sucking us," the Lizard King mocked. His men laughed.

"*Two!*" Pedro shouted. Then to Dave he whispered out of the corner of his mouth, "Why aren't they moving?"

"I don't know," Dave said. "But you'd better decide what you're going to do before you get to three."

"*Three*!" Pedro shouted. "Now get going before I come over there," he said hopefully.

The Lizard King didn't move. He just smiled. "Who are you really, Pedro? Tell me, tell the town."

Pedro was shocked and glanced at the townspeople who had gathered at the commotion, they all looked a little confused. The mayor stepped forward.

"This is El Chupacabra," he said pointing at Pedro. "And I am warning you, Lizard King, you had better leave town before he goes crazy."

Pedro gulped.

The Lizard King laughed harder than ever, then stopped abruptly. "Enough of this nonsense. Bring him out." He said gesturing to Gary Gecko.

The small lizard nodded, skittered to a wagon, and climbed in. Two wooden planks came sliding out of the back, making a ramp, and Gecko pushed down a wheel chair. In it, tied and gagged, was a most hideous creature. Its red eyes fixed firmly on Pedro. Pedro swallowed hard, for there was no mistaking the real El Chupacabra.

At the sight of the monstrosity in the wheel chair, there was a gasp from the crowd. Bonita looked at Pedro, scared and confused.

"I am sorry," he whispered.

"This is the real El Chupacabra," the Lizard King said, addressing the crowd.

The mayor turned to Pedro. "What's going on?"

"Yes, Pedro,"—the Lizard King smirked—"tell us what's going on. Who are you really?"

"I am a dog," Pedro said quietly, his head bent in shame.

"A *dog*!" the Lizard King bellowed.

Pedro turned to Bonita to explain but stopped when he saw her crying.

"Oh, Pedro, how could you?" she said and ran over to her father who consoled her and looked at Pedro in disappointment.

"Well, mutt, I think you have caused quite enough trouble round here. It's time you left," the Lizard King said.

El Chupacabra started struggling wildly, his chair bouncing up and down. He chewed at his muzzle and bit through it in no time.

"You promised me I could eat him!" he screeched at the king.

"Ha, I am not going to untie you. Look what you did to my eye last time we met. No, you can stay in your chair."

El Chupacabra was furious; he shook and twisted in his chair, biting at the ropes restraining him.

"Quick, make sure he doesn't get out of that chair," the Lizard King ordered his men.

But it was too late. An ear splitting howl filled the night air as El Chupacabra broke free. El Chupacabra picked up the wheel chair and threw it across the square, smashing it to pieces.

"Now you are mine!" El Chupacabra screamed at Pedro.

"Pedro, run," Dave shouted.

"No," Pedro said, "this is it."

"This is what? What are you talking about? You got to run, Pedro. It's your only chance," Dave pleaded.

"No, I am the bravest dog in Mexico," Pedro said, lifting his head up high. "I made a promise—I would not run and hide or cry like a puppy, and I would always protect my pack even with my life."

"Pedro, *no*, no, your mother wouldn't have wanted this. If you don't run, El Chupacabra will kill you. You don't stand a chance against this monster."

But Pedro was not listening. He stayed, and he faced El Chupacabra.

Chapter 16—The Showdown

"So you are not a coward, but you are stupid. I am going to pull your head off and ..."

Before El Chupacabra could finish, Pedro ran at full speed, leaping at El Chupacabra's chest, knocking him over. Pedro quickly rolled onto his feet and pounced on the monster's hideous head, sinking his teeth into the soft flesh of his cheek. El Chupacabra jumped up howling and swiping at Pedro with his sharp claws, but Pedro was too quick. He dodged the claws and bit into El Chupacabra's ear, shaking it until it began to tear. El Chupacabra screamed again. Dave could barely watch but shouted, "Look out" as another claw came. Pedro quickly moved down to El Chupacabra's shoulder, biting into his neck. The beast stumbled, flailing his arms wildly. El Chupacabra grabbed Pedro's tail and began to pull him off.

Dave screamed, "His nipples Pedro. Grab his nipples."

Pedro stretched out his head and firmly gripped a nipple with his wonky teeth, giving it a vicious shake. El Chupacabra howled, letting go of Pedro's tail, grabbed him by the throat, and ripped him off his now throbbing nipple."

AAaaaaaggghhhh," he screamed in a war cry and landed two vicious blows to Pedro's head. Pedro yelped in pain, but El Chupacabra was not finished. He brought his knee up and smashed it into the side of Pedro's head several times, then shook him violently before throwing his still body down with a sickening thud.

Bonita screamed and would have run to Pedro, but her father held her back.

Dave scrambled onto Pedro's nose. "Noooooooo," he cried in anguish looking at Pedro's closed, bloodied eyes.

El Chupacabra raised his arms and shook his fists at the sky.

"Aaaagghhh," he cried in pain. "My nipple is killing me. That's it! You are all dead; I am going to suck everyone's brains out. And you are first," he said pointing at Bonita.

Even the Lizard King and his gang thought this was taking things a bit far, but everyone was too scared to do anything. El Chupacabra moved towards Bonita.

Suddenly Pedro jumped up and threw himself onto El Chupacabra's back, catching him by surprise and knocking him off balance. El Chupacabra stumbled towards the well, grabbing the side with his claws. Pedro quickly clambered over El Chupacabra's shoulders and onto his chest.

"No, no, not the nipples again," El Chupacabra pleaded and quickly covered them with his claws.

Pedro saw his chance and dropped to the floor. Grabbing the beast by an ankle, he tipped him over and into the well. El Chupacabra tried to grab the wall again, but missed. His legs flailed wildly as he toppled over, kicking Pedro violently and sending him sprawling.

"Fluuuuuuffffffff," El Chupacabra cried, before a dull thud silenced him.

Pedro lay there motionless. Bonita ran to him, knelt at his side, and cried as she looked at his battered body.

The Lizard King saw his chance. "Finish him," he commanded his followers.

But the lizard gang didn't move.

"Finish him," he demanded.

Gary Gecko looked at the Lizard King in disgust. "We've seen enough." He said shaking his head.

The lizard gang silently mounted their spiders and left town, stopping only briefly to tip their hats to Bonita.

The furious Lizard King stormed towards Pedro. "If you want something done right, do it yourself," he muttered.

Just then a rock hit him in the side of the head. "Aaaarrgghh, who threw that?"

"I did," said Señor Hables stepping forward.

"Right! First I will deal with you and then this mutt," the Lizard King said, turning towards him. A large possum standing next to the mayor, picked up a rock, and threw it at the Lizard King, barely missing him.

"Hey!" The king shouted. "What do you think you are doing?"

The mayor stepped forward and shouted "Get out of our town,"

A young anteater picked up a rock and threw it hard at the Lizard King, striking him on the chest

"Get out!" She yelled.

Then more townspeople stepped forward, throwing whatever they could lay their hands on—rocks, sticks, even some locusts.

"Hey, hey, hey!" the Lizard King said as he ducked and weaved, trying to avoid the missiles.

"You haven't seen the last of me," he shouted as he ran out of town pursued by a group of angry squirrels armed with nuts.

The townspeople cheered in triumph as the Lizard King disappeared, but the jubilation was short lived; they turned back to where Bonita was holding Pedro's limp head in her lap.

"Oh Papá, quick get the doctor, Pedro is hurt real bad."

Chapter 17—Good Dogs Go To Heaven

"Hey look he's opening his eyes," Dave said jumping up and down in excitement.

"How long have I been out?" Pedro sat up, groaning at the soreness of his muscles and the stiffness of his joints.

"Two days. For a while there, pal, we didn't think you were going to make it, but you had a great nurse."

Pedro saw Bonita standing by the door. She looked tired.

"Why didn't you tell me you had fleas?" she demanded.

"What?" Pedro didn't know what to say.

Bonita smiled, ran over, giving him big sloppy lick. "Just kidding, welcome back to the land of the living."

"I take it that you have met Dave then," Pedro said.

"Yes, Dave has not left your side. He did get kind of hungry, though, so I had to let him … well you know." Bonita gave her head a scratch.

"She's a keeper," Dave said rubbing his tummy.

"I am sorry for not telling you the truth," Pedro said.

"It's okay. I know you tried, but no more secrets."

"I promise."

"Now rest and get your strength back. I will go tell Papá and the rest of town that you are awake. They have been very worried and are waiting for news." Bonita gave Pedro another lick before she left.

"What happened to the Lizard King?" Pedro asked Dave.

"The townsfolk ran him off. After you were knocked out they turned on him, throwing anything they could find at him. You would have been proud of your pack."

"And El Chupacabra?" Pedro slowly got to his feet.

"Oh, he is still down the well. He says he likes it down there."

Pedro walked over to the window and looked at the well surrounded by red tape and warning signs. "Isn't the mayor worried he will get out?"

"No, he told the Mayor he is sick of all that craziness. He just wants to retire. Now that he has been finally defeated he says he is no longer El Chupacabra! His real name is Fred."

"Fred?" Pedro said in surprise.

"Yeah, and Fred says that now he has been vanquished, you are El Chupacabra."

"What are you chatting about? I can't be El Chupacabra. I'm a dog."

"Well, Fred says that's the way it has been for hundreds of years. El Chupacabra is a tradition, and there have been many El Chupacabras over the years, some good, some bad ... and some a little crazy, like Fred."

Pedro got his sheriffs hat and put it on. "Hmm, Sheriff El Chupacabra. It kind of has a ring to it, don't you think?"

From the street Pedro heard voices, and he went over to the window. Gathered below was the entire town. They cheered when they saw Pedro.

When the cheering died down, the mayor shouted, "Will you stay and be Sheriff El Chupacabra?"

"Yes," Pedro said, "but I will be a good El Chupacabra. Where there is injustice, El Chupacabra will bring justice. Where there is wrong doing, El Chupacabra will bring... err, right doing. Where there is dark, El Chupacabra will bring light ..."

"Hey, don't overdo it dork." Dave whispered in Pedro's ear.

"Oh, okay," he answered, then raised his voice once more. "I will protect Santa Maria with my life."

The townsfolk went wild, cheering and whooping. When Nigel the goat made his way to the front, the crowd settled down and parted to give him room.

"If you are now El Chupacabra, does this mean you will be sucking goats?" Nigel asked.

Pedro held up his paws. "No, no, I think that's just something Fred did."

"Oh, okay, that's good then," Nigel said nodding his head.

"What now, Sheriff El Chupacabra?" Bonita shouted.

"Well, every El Chupacabra needs a good woman," Pedro said.

Bonita blushed as the crowd responded with a loud, "Woooooooh."

"But first," Pedro announced, "I must rescue my mother." He turned to Dave. "Okay partner, let's ride."

The End

Papa G welcomes feedback and can be contacted at heypapa.g@gmail.com

75295807R00035

Made in the USA
Middletown, DE
04 June 2018